© 1996 Geddes & Grosset Ltd
Published by Geddes & Grosset Ltd,
New Lanark, Scotland.

ISBN 1 85534 163 8

Printed and bound in Slovenia

The Fir Tree

Retold by Judy Hamilton
Illustrated by Liz Sawyer

Tarantula Books

The little Fir Tree had a good place to live, out in the fresh air and sunlight of the forest, surrounded by many other fir trees of all sizes. But the Fir Tree was not happy. It was not interested in its pleasant surroundings. When children playing in the forest stopped to admire its pretty, dainty branches, it paid no attention. The little Fir Tree spent its days wishing to grow bigger.

"I want to be a great tree, with a view over all the world," it said. "I want to nod gracefully in the wind and have birds nesting in my branches!"

Three years passed, with all the beauty of one season following another, but still the Fir Tree took no notice of the good life that it had. It had grown tall, sure enough, but now it wanted to grow old.

In the autumn, the Fir Tree watched the woodcutters come and fell the biggest trees; they stripped their branches and carried them away. In spring, the swallows came and told the Fir Tree that the big trees were used as masts for ships that sailed far away to Egypt. The Fir Tree wanted to go too.

"Enjoy your young life while you have it," said the Sun, but the Fir Tree did not understand.

At Christmas time, the woodcutters chopped down younger trees. Still restless, the Fir Tree asked the sparrows where these trees were going.

"They are placed in the windows of the houses in the town and decorated and dressed up with candles and baubles," the sparrows said.

"That sounds even better than going across the sea!" exclaimed the Fir Tree. "I can't wait for next Christmas. I would so love to look grand like that. Better things would happen then."

"Take time to enjoy us while you are young," said the Air and the Sunshine. But the Fir Tree was too busy wishing for other things.

The Fir Tree grew even taller and more handsome. The next Christmas, it was the first tree to be felled. As it felt the sharp blade of the axe cut through its trunk, it suddenly realised that it would miss its happy home in the forest with the other trees and the birds and animals. It felt sad.

The Fir Tree was taken in a wagon with some other trees to a yard.

"Perfect!" said a man's voice. "We'll have this one!" And the Fir Tree was taken to a big house and set in a tub in the window of a beautiful sitting room. What would happen now?

The children and the servants of the house decorated the Fir Tree with every kind of bauble and with toys, sweets, apples, nuts and hundreds of little candles. At the top they fixed a silver star. It looked magnificent.

But the Fir Tree was still not content. How it longed for evening to come when the candles would be lit! And then what would happen? The Fir Tree could hardly bear the waiting.

At last it grew dark and the candles were lit. The Fir Tree looked beautiful, but when it moved, the candles would scorch its branches. The Fir Tree was frightened now.

The Fir Tree stood very still, too frightened to move, and watched as all the people of the house came into the room. They all stopped to admire it, and the children danced around it.

Then the children rushed at the Fir Tree. What were they doing? They were tearing off all the toys and sweets. They were breaking its branches! All the candles were put out, and it was stripped bare. Only the silver star remained.

Then all the children gathered round one old man and begged him for a story.

"What do I do now?" wondered the Fir Tree. But they had finished with it.

The old man told the story of Klumpey Dumpey. Klumpey Dumpey fell down the stairs but became an honourable man and married a princess.

The Fir Tree thought it was a lovely story. "Perhaps something like that will happen to me," it thought. "Perhaps I shall marry a princess! Oh, I can't wait until tomorrow comes. Then I shall be decorated again. I shall stand ever so still and then I shall enjoy looking splendid!"

But when morning came, the Fir Tree was not decorated again. Instead, it was taken up into the attic.

It was dark and quiet in the attic. Nobody came there. The Fir Tree had plenty of time to think. What was to become of it now?

"It's winter outside," thought the Fir Tree. "There is snow and ice on the ground. They have put me here to wait for spring, when I can be planted again. That will be nice. I just wish that it wasn't so dark and lonely! The snow was pretty in the forest, and I had the animals and birds for company."

Then one day, some mice came to find warmth in the Fir Tree's branches. They were friendly and inquisitive.

"Tell us about yourself," they said to the Fir Tree.

So the Fir Tree began to tell the little mice about the forest and the sunshine and the birdsong.

"How happy you must have been," said the mice.

"Yes, I suppose I was happy, come to think of it," said the Fir Tree.

Then it told the mice all about Christmas, when it had been decorated so splendidly.

"What a wonderful time you must have had, Old Fir Tree," said the mice.

"I suppose it was," said the Fir Tree," but I am not old, you know!"

The next night the mice came back with more of their friends. The Fir Tree told them all about its life and then it told them the story of Klumpey Dumpey. The more it talked, the more it remembered how happy it was before. But still it hoped for better things to come. "Klumpey Dumpey fell downstairs and yet he married a princess," said the Fir Tree. "Perhaps one day I may marry a princess too!"

The mice liked the story of Klumpey Dumpey very much. Each night they would bring more of their friends to hear it. One night, two rats came to join them, but the rats were not impressed.

"Don't you know any other stories?" asked the rats. "What about the story of the storeroom where you go in thin and come out fat?"

The Fir Tree shook its head. It only knew the story of Klumpey Dumpey. So the rats left, and soon after that the mice got bored and stopped coming. The Fir Tree missed the company of the cheerful little creatures.

"It was nice having them to talk to," it said, "but those days are past now. It will be nice to get out again. I shall make the most of it this time."

Springtime came and the Fir Tree was taken out at last into the courtyard. It was a beautiful spring day and the Fir Tree rejoiced in it.

It tried to spread out its branches in the sunshine, but they were brown and withered! Some children came and trod on it as it lay there.

"Ugly tree!" they said, and stamped on it.

The Fir Tree looked at itself and realised that its life was at an end.

"If only I had enjoyed my youth while I had it!" it sighed.

A servant came and chopped the Fir Tree into pieces. With each chop, it remembered the happy times it had had but which it had never taken the time to enjoy.

The Fir Tree was burned. Soon nothing remained except the silver star—which it had worn on the happiest day of its life—the life that was now past.